Text copyright © 1996 by Kate Banks

Pictures copyright © 1996 by Georg Hallensleben

Originally published in French under the title *Araignée, Petite Araignée,*

copyright © 1996 by Editions Gallimard

All rights reserved

Published simultaneously in Canada by HarperCollinsCanadaLtd

Printed in Italy

First American edition, 1996

Library of Congress Cataloging-in-Publication Data

Banks, Kate.

[Araignée, petite araignée]

Spider, spider / Kate Banks ; pictures by Georg Hallensleben. — 1st American ed.

p.    cm.

"Frances Foster books."

[1. Spiders—Fiction.  2. Imagination—Fiction.  3. Mothers and sons—Fiction.]

I. Hallensleben, Georg, ill.  II. Title.

PZ7.B22594Sp    1996    [E]—dc20    96-11653 CIP AC

# SPIDER SPIDER

## Kate Banks · Pictures by Georg Hallensleben

**Frances Foster Books**

**Farrar, Straus and Giroux · New York**

Peter watched a spider crawl across the floor.
It was small, green, and furry.
"I will become a spider,"
said Peter.

"Oh, you will?" said his mother.
"And what will you do?"

"I will crawl up the chair and onto the table. And when you are not looking I will drink from your glass and eat crumbs from your plate," said Peter.

"Then I will brush you
from the table onto the
floor," said Peter's mother.
"And I will sweep you out the door."

"I will crawl back up the door and through the keyhole," said Peter. "I will wait until you are sleeping, and I will crawl into your bed and bite your toe."

"Then I will put you in the bathtub, and I will turn on the shower," said Peter's mother.

"Spiders don't like baths," said Peter.

"Then you will slide down the drain and
into the sewer, where it is dark and wet."

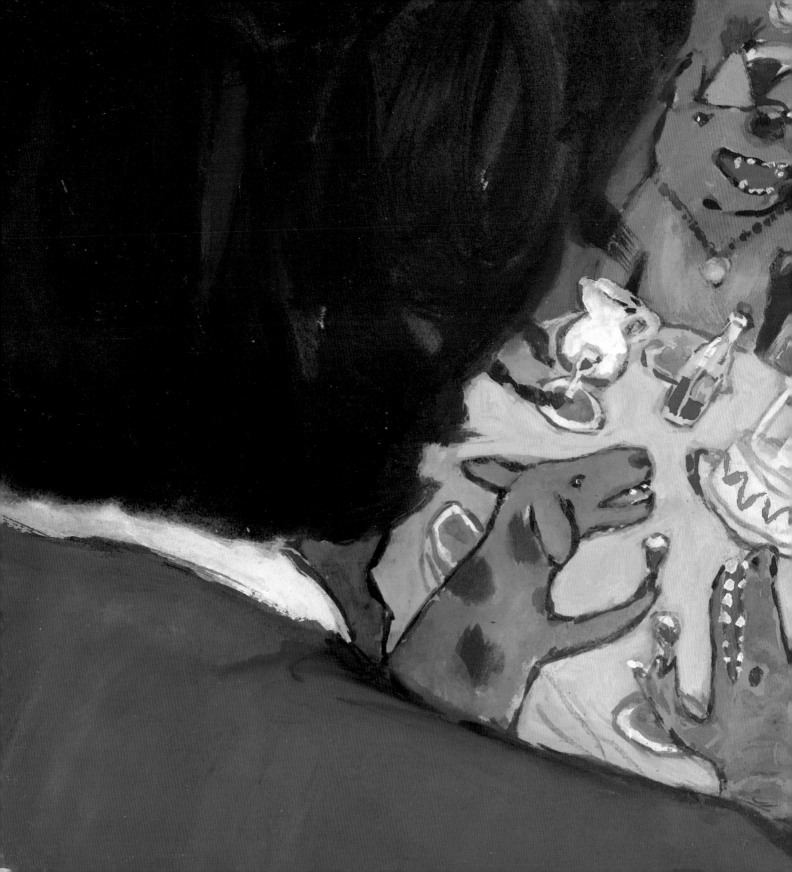

"But I am small," said Peter. "I will climb out of the sewer, up the wall, and back in your window. I will crawl onto the book you are reading, and I will fall asleep."

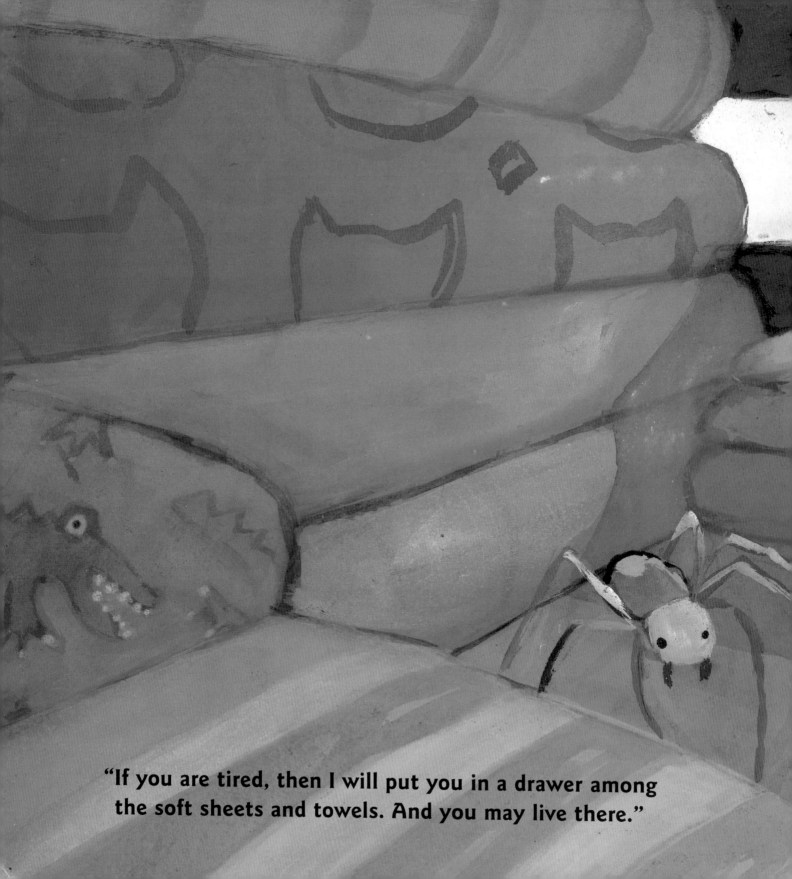

"If you are tired, then I will put you in a drawer among the soft sheets and towels. And you may live there."

"I will take a nap," said Peter. "But when I wake up I will crawl out of the drawer. I will climb up your leg and into your pocket."

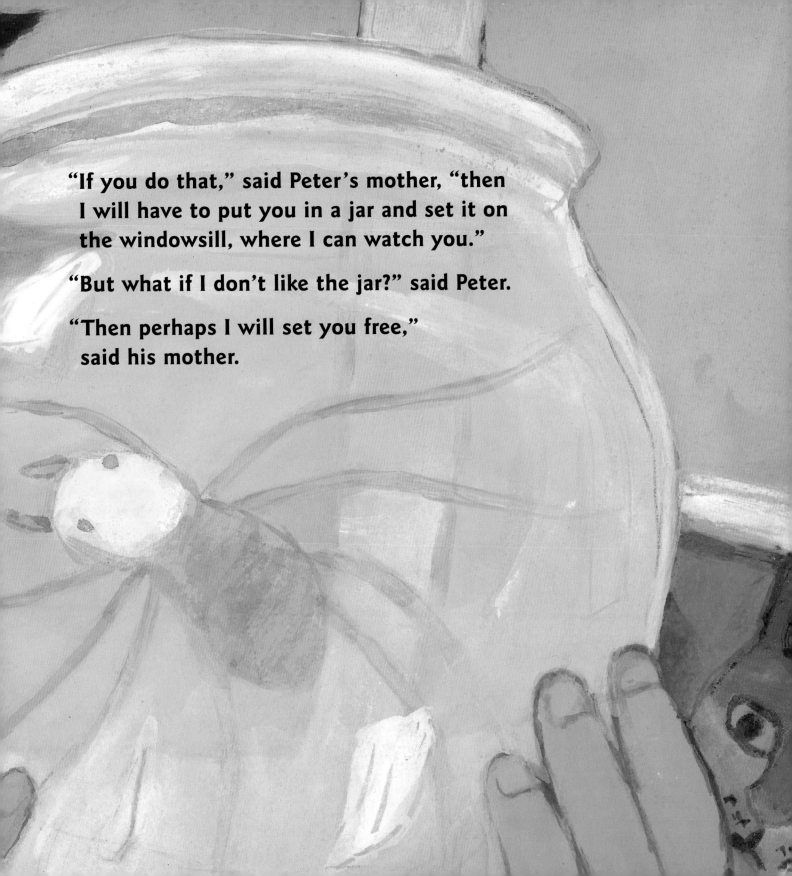

"If you do that," said Peter's mother, "then I will have to put you in a jar and set it on the windowsill, where I can watch you."

"But what if I don't like the jar?" said Peter.

"Then perhaps I will set you free," said his mother.

"If you set me free," said Peter,
"I will climb onto your arm and I
will hide in your sleeve."

"When I find you," said Peter's mother, "I will shake you from my sleeve."

"And what will you do then?" asked Peter.

"I will become a spider, too," said Peter's mother.